Dear Parent:
Your child's love of reading starts here!

Every child learns to read in a different way and at his or her own speed. Some go back and forth between reading levels and read favorite books again and again. Others read through each level in order. You can help your young reader improve and become more confident by encouraging his or her own interests and abilities. From books your child reads with you to the first books he or she reads alone, there are I Can Read Books for every stage of reading:

SHARED READING
Basic language, word repetition, and whimsical illustrations, ideal for sharing with your emergent reader

BEGINNING READING
Short sentences, familiar words, and simple concepts for children eager to read on their own

READING WITH HELP
Engaging stories, longer sentences, and language play for developing readers

READING ALONE
Complex plots, challenging vocabulary, and high-interest topics for the independent reader

ADVANCED READING
Short paragraphs, chapters, and exciting themes for the perfect bridge to chapter books

I Can Read Books have introduced children to the joy of reading since 1957. Featuring award-winning authors and illustrators and a fabulous cast of beloved characters, I Can Read Books set the standard for beginning readers.

A lifetime of discovery begins with the magical words "I Can Read!"

Visit www.icanread.com for information
on enriching your child's reading experience.

For Cody and Troy.
Just be yourselves!
—R.S.

I Can Read Book® is a trademark of HarperCollins Publishers.

Splat the Cat with a Bang and a Clang
Copyright © 2013 by Rob Scotton
All rights reserved. Printed in the United States of America.
No part of this book may be used or reproduced in any manner whatsoever without written permission except in the case of brief quotations embodied in critical articles and reviews. For information address HarperCollins Children's Books, a division of HarperCollins Publishers, 10 East 53rd Street, New York, NY 10022.
www.icanread.com

Library of Congress Cataloging-in-Publication Data is available.
ISBN 978-0-06-209021-8 (trade bdg.) —ISBN 978-0-06-209019-5 (pbk.)

13 14 15 16 LP/WOR 10 9 8 7 6 5 4 3 2 ❖ First Edition

Splat the Cat
with a Bang and a Clang

Based on the bestselling books by Rob Scotton

Cover art by Rick Farley

Text by Amy Hsu Lin

Interior illustrations by Robert Eberz

HARPER

An Imprint of HarperCollinsPublishers

Splat the cat

watched his friends' band

play in Spike's dad's garage.

"Welcome, Splat,
and all you cool cats!"
called Kitten.
"We're the Cat Gang!"

Spike hit the drum

with a *bang, bang, bang,*

and Plank plucked the guitar

with a *twang, twang, twang,*

while Kitten softly sang.

Splat clapped when they finished.

The Cat Gang bowed,

but then Kitten frowned.

Something was missing.

"You're one of us, Splat,"
said Kitten.

"That's true.
You should play, too," said Spike.
"The Cat Gang doesn't feel right
without you," said Plank.

"But I can't play an instrument,"
said Splat.
"And I never did get the hang
of singing!"

"You'll think of something," said Spike.

"Right," Plank said.

But nothing sprang to mind.

"Try using your head," said Kitten.

So Splat poked his head into a box.

He found an old car horn

and a fancy coat. "Aha!" Splat said.

He waited for his turn to play.

Spike went *bang*.

Plank went *twang*.

Kitten sang.

And Splat went . . .

HONK!

"Sorry," said Splat.

"Maybe if you use your head

in a different way," Kitten said.

"Okay," said Splat.

Splat reached up to scratch his head

and bumped into an old bell

that was hanging on the wall.

"Aha!" Splat said.

He waited for his turn to play.

18

Spike drummed. *Bang, bang.*

Plank plucked. *Twang, twang.*

Kitten sang.

Splat rang. *Ding, ding!*

Splat shook his head.

"That's still not the right sound

for the Cat Gang," he said.

20

"Sorry," said Spike.

"Too bad," said Plank.

With a pang of sadness,

Splat turned to leave.

"Wait, Splat," Kitten said.

"I know what you can do.

You can dance!"

"Dance?" said Splat.

"Sure!" Spike said.

"Right on!" said Plank.

So the Cat Gang began to play,

and Splat began to dance.

Splat had so much fun dancing
that he forgot to watch his feet.
He tripped on a wrench.

Then he kicked the bell.

Ding!

Then he sat on the car horn.

Honk!

The noise startled Splat.

He sprang up in the air.

His head banged into big metal cans.

CLANG!

The music stopped.

"Oops!" said Splat.

Kitten smiled.

"Wow, you really did use your head,"
she said.

"That sound was perfect
for the Cat Gang!
Do it again."

Splat rubbed his head.

"Okay, but this time

I won't use my head."

He picked up the wrench.

On the night of the show,

Spike hit the drum

with a *bang, bang, bang.*

Plank plucked the guitar

with a *twang, twang, twang.*

Kitten softly sang,
and Splat struck the can
with a *clang, clang, clang.*
The crowd cheered
and clapped wildly.

And this time,

the whole Cat Gang

took a bow together.